Fish Story

PARENTS' MAGAZINE BOOK CLUBS, INC.

Fish Story

by Robert Tallon

10 9 8 7 6 5 4 3 2 1

Library of Congress Cataloging in Publication Data

Tallon, Robert, 1939-
Fish story.

SUMMARY: A small fish who wants to see the
world beyond his pond is befriended by a cat who has
other plans for the voyager.
[1. Fishes—Fiction] I. Title.
PZ7.T157Fi   [E]   76-23092
ISBN 0-03-017526-7

For my brothers, Charles and Bill.

"I've got to get out of here!"
Little Fish said.
"I'm tired of swimming in the
same water.
I want a bigger pond."
Big Cat, strolling by, heard him.

"Can I be of help?" Big Cat asked.
"I want to see the world,"
Little Fish said.
"The world is beautiful up here,
really beautiful," Big Cat said.
"The flowers...the trees...the ocean
just over the hill."

"Ocean! Old Fish told me about
the ocean," Little Fish said.
"Can you take me there?"
"Of course," said Big Cat.
"But first, I'll have to go home
and get a bag to carry you in."
"Please hurry, back," Little Fish said.

Big Cat returned with a large
plastic bag.
He lowered it into the water.
Little Fish swam inside.
"Thank you," Little Fish said.
"I'll repay you for your kindness
one day."
"No need to. Glad to help a friend,"
Big Cat said, licking his lips.

Big Cat ran through the woods.
"How beautiful...is that a flower?"
Little Fish asked.
"Yeah, that's a flower," Big Cat said.
"Is that a bird?"
"Yeah," Big Cat snarled.
"Could we stop?" Little Fish asked.
"No," Big Cat yelled.
"Where is the ocean?" Little Fish
asked.
"Just over the hill," Big Cat said.
"Now, be quiet! You're asking too
many questions."
"I'm sorry," Little Fish said,
"but it's so new to me."

Big Cat ran over the hill
and into a shabby house. "Is the ocean
in here?" Little Fish asked.
"Your trip is over," Big Cat said.
Little Fish looked around at the pots
and pans hanging on the walls.
"Is…is…this your pond?" She asked.
"No…It's my kitchen, stupid Fish,"
Big Cat said.
"And I'm going to cook you!"

Little Fish shook and trembled.
"Why me?" she asked.
Big Cat sang to himself
as he greased a frying pan with his paw.
"Didn't Old Fish ever tell you
about Cats and Fishes?" he asked.
"Are you...a...Cat?" Little Fish asked.
"Yes, Big Cat's the name.
And I'm going to eat you...
nothing personal."

"But I'm all bones," Little Fish cried.
"Quiet! I'm trying to read this
cookbook,"
Big Cat said.
"Hmm...boiled...baked...
creamed with almonds...
Here it is! Fried fish with pickles,
mayonnaise, banana tips, ketchup
and mustard. I'm starved!"
"Big Cat, wait, please!" Little Fish
yelled.
"Just look at me. I'm all bones.
I'd be just a snack for you.
But I know a Big Fish...so big,
he'd fill this kitchen."

Big Cat looked at Little Fish.
"Just where is this big fish?" he asked.
"Back at the pond.
He's big enough to last you a month,"
Little Fish said.
"If you take me back, I'll get him
for you."
"How?" Big Cat asked.
"Have you got some ketchup?" Little
Fish asked.
"What if I do?" Big Cat answered.
"He just loves ketchup."
"He does, eh? Big Cat asked.
"Just take me back," Little Fish said.
"Bring a string, some ketchup,
and leave the rest to me."

Big Cat took up the bag with
Little Fish and another bag with the
ketchup and raced back to the pond.

He dropped Little Fish inside,
then lowered the string with
the ketchup.
Little Fish swam out of the bag.
"How wonderful to be back in my
beautiful pond," he thought
as he swam around and around.

Big Cat jiggled the string.
"Hurry up, Little Fish, get your
dopey friend.
I'm starved!" he said.
Little Fish grabbed the string
and swam down with it.
"Okay, Big Cat," Little Fish called.
"Pull it up!"
Big Cat pulled on the string.
He pulled and pulled—

—and landed his catch.
"You tricked me," Big Cat yelled,
jumping up and down.
Little Fish laughed as he swam
to the center of the pond.
"It was just a Fish Story," he sang out.
"Just a Fish Story…for a Big Cat!"

About the Author

Robert Tallon is a highly successful commercial artist in a wide variety of media, including television. His drawings appear on the covers, of, among others, the *New Yorker* and *Time* magazine. He is the author/illustrator of several books, including *Rotten Kidphabets* and *Zag: A Search Through the Alphabet*. His *Rhoda's Restaurant* received the Brooklyn Art Books for Children Citation for 1975, given by the Brooklyn Museum.

About the Book

The full-color art was camera-separated for printing by offset.
The art is pen-and-ink with watercolor.
The Text and display are set in Bookman.